To Nicole Mandrell Shipley,
an answer to a mother's prayers.
And to Clint and Rance Collins,
the godchildren who have
blessed my life beyond compare.
LOUISE

For my sons, Clint and Rance,
who have taught me that
a parent's smiles and tears
are the most precious
of all of God's gifts.
ACE

To all the children
who will touch this book,
may your childhood
be filled with love.
LOUISE AND ACE

Sunrise Over The Harbor

Sunrise Over

Louise Mandrell and Ace Collins

Children's Holiday Adventure Series

Volume 11

THE SUMMIT GROUP
1227 West Magnolia, Suite 500, Fort Worth, Texas 76104

Printed in the United States of America.

93 10 9 8 7 6 5 4 3 2 1

Jacket and Book Design by Cheryl Corbitt

LIBRARY OF CONGRESS CATALOGING-IN-PUBLICATION DATA
Mandrell, Louise.
Sunrise over the harbor / Louise Mandrell and Ace Collins; illustrated by Mark Gale.
p. cm. – (Louise Mandrell & Ace Collins holiday adventure series; v. 11)
Summary: In 1814 Nathan Dunn, a ten-year-old cabin boy serving on an American ship, meets Francis Scott Key during the great naval battle at Fort McHenry and becomes a hero.
ISBN 1-56530-040-8: $12.95
1. United States – History – War of 1812 – Juvenile fiction. [1. United States – History – War of 1812 – Fiction. 2. Key, Francis Scott, 1779-1843 – Fiction.] I. Collins, Ace. II. Gale, Mark, ill. III. Title. IV. Series: Mandrell, Louise. Louise Mandrell & Ace Collins holiday adventure series; v. 11.
PZ7. M31254Su 1993
[Fic] – dc20 93-310
CIP
AC

The Harbor

Illustrated by Mark Gale

THE SUMMIT GROUP

"There will be a huge battle tonight," shouted the sailor toward the cabin boy.

Glancing up from his work, Nathan Dunn asked, "How can you be so sure, sir?"

Walking over to where the thirteen-year-old sat on the deck of the small frigate ship, the young officer took off his three-cornered hat, wiped his brow, and inspected the way Nathan was wrapping the lengths of rope. "You are doing a good job. You will make a good seaman, but I think you will be an even better artist."

Grinning proudly, Nathan continued to work with the line as George Chapman watched. Concentrating on his task, the lad didn't look up again until the man spoke.

"Do you have paper and quill?" he inquired. "And plenty of ink?"

"Yes," Nathan responded. "The captain brought me some yesterday. Do you really think there is going to be a big battle tonight?"

"One of the biggest of the war," Chapman solemnly stated. "Our spies have informed us that the British are going to attack Fort McHenry and try to bring down the city of Baltimore. They are waiting until nightfall when they will have the cover of darkness. I fear that there will be a great many things for you to draw this evening, and not all of them good. I pray that one of your sketches will show an American victory. Yet, the British fleet is here in force, and that great force might bring us to our knees."

Nathan listened intently to the young officer's words, but he said nothing. He didn't understand the reasons for the war, nor could he comprehend the hatred that the British and Americans seemed to have for one another. Within the past few months Nathan had witnessed several battles, seen many men die, and observed the destruction that is a part of war. The more he saw of war, the less he understood it. Was this bloodshed worth it? He didn't see how, but it was not his place to comment. He was simply to go with Mr. Chapman and do as he was told.

Chapman was grateful to have the lad. He had no family; they had died in the early part of the war. Until he met and befriended young Nathan, he was lonely and bitter. Looking out for Nathan had given him a purpose and a reason to fight.

When Chapman was transferred to this prisoner exchange ship, he arranged for Nathan to come with him, and the young officer became the unofficial guardian of the sandy-haired orphan. It was George who had discovered the lad's artistic talent, and he had used a part of his own meager savings to purchase paper, ink, pen, and paints for Nathan. Now all the sailors came by to watch the lad draw. Many of them had sent his paintings and sketches home to their families. Even the captain encouraged Nathan's efforts.

"Launch approaching," a watchman called out.

"Looks like we have some company," George Chapman smiled. "I wonder who it could be."

Jumping up from the deck, Nathan joined the officer as he walked quickly astern. Staring out over the waves, they watched a small boat being rowed up to their own. Aboard it were several British seamen, as well as three other men. One was an American officer; the other two were dressed in civilian clothes.

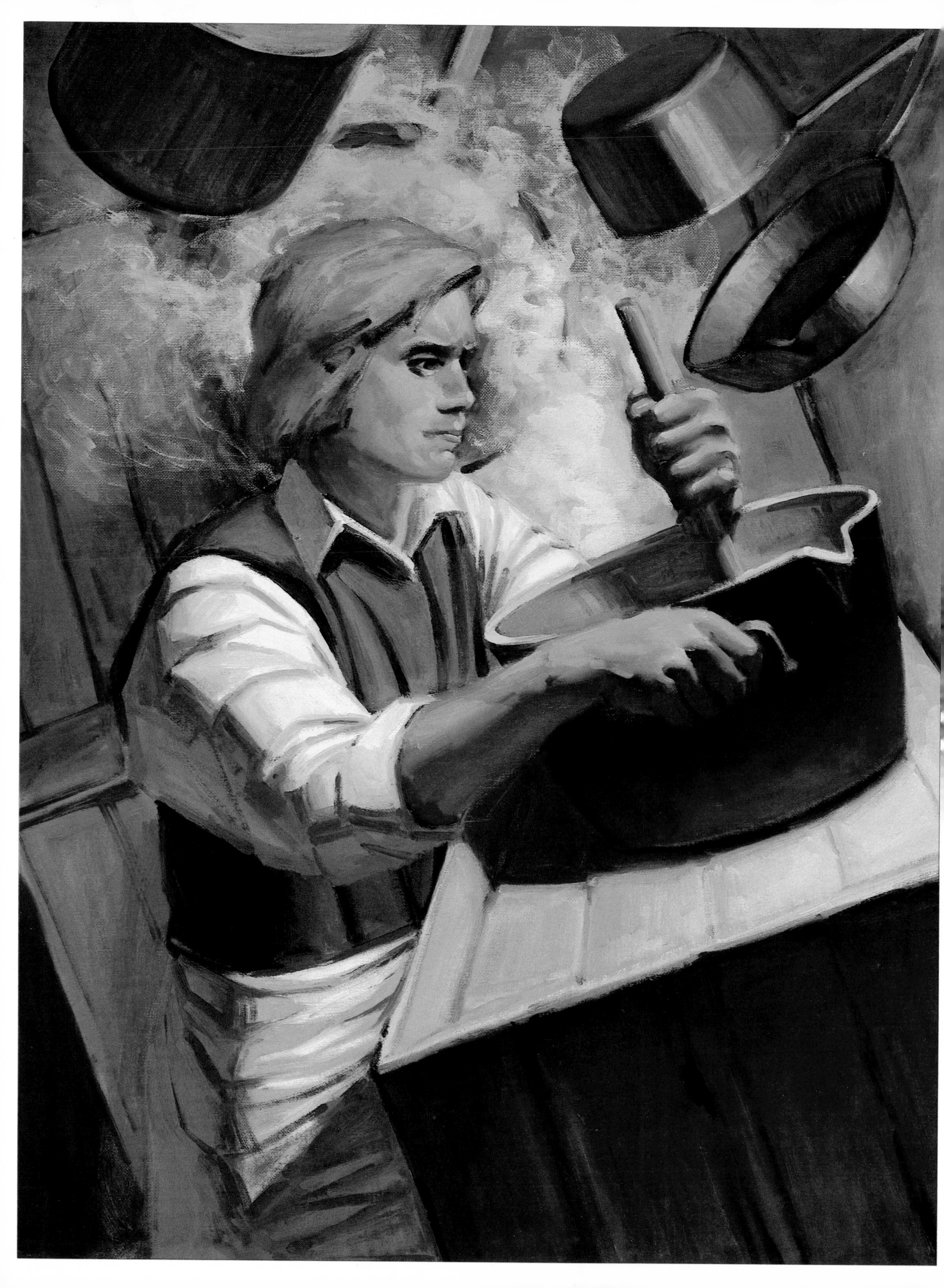

"Colonel J. S. Skinner," Chapman remarked as the small boat's passengers began their climb onto their frigate.

"Who is he?" Nathan asked.

"An officer who is said to be a friend of President Madison," the sailor explained. "This other man must be important also."

"What about the British sailors?" Nathan questioned.

"They came under a flag of truce," Chapman answered, "so we don't have to worry about them. Besides, this is an exchange ship, so they are probably just dropping those two off to trade for some of their men."

Scratching his brow, Chapman mused, "Strange, I didn't hear about Colonel Skinner being captured."

The lad and sailor watched the boat unload its occupants, push off, and head back into the harbor. "You go back to work," Chapman ordered, "and I'll try to solve this little mystery."

Over the course of the next few hours, Nathan saw little of Mr. Chapman. He went about his assignments, served the captain his dinner, and then returned to the deck to wait for the first signs of the battle. As the sun began to set, Fort McHenry, looking insignificant and small, caught the lad's attention. He couldn't believe that the hopes of Baltimore, maybe even the whole country, depended on this outpost. Picking up his paper and quill, he began to draw the fort. As he sketched, he wondered what would be left of it by the next morning.

He had been at work on his drawing for an hour when he heard a deep voice say, "That is a fine drawing."

Looking up, Nathan stared into the dark blue eyes of the civilian who had been brought on board the frigate by the British sailors. The lad nodded shyly, rose to his feet, and stood saluting the stranger.

Smiling, the tall, distinguished gentleman shook his head and signalled for the cabin boy to relax. "I am not an officer," he laughed, "so you don't have to salute me. As a matter of fact, the best thing I probably am is a father. I have a couple of children about your age. What is your name, son?"

"Nathan Dunn, sir," the boy replied.

"Your drawing of our fort is very good," he observed. "Could I see it?"

Picking up the sketch, Nathan handed it to the visitor. The man studied it for a few seconds, nodded his head in approval, and sighed, "Let us pray that the flag that you have drawn so beautifully over the fort is still there in the morning." Returning the sketch, the man walked over to the side of the ship and stared out into the harbor. He stayed there for some time, observing the activity, before turning back to Nathan.

"My name is Francis Scott Key," he introduced himself. He went on, "Tonight I fear for the lives of my family. I have not seen them in more than a week, and the British have the firepower to win this battle. If they do, I wonder about the fate of my wife and two children."

Nathan had grown accustomed to the rough talk of sailing men. A man expressing love and compassion was something he rarely saw. He was moved by the man's open display of concern, and he felt himself drawn to him.

"Mr. Key," the boy said, "we will win. I know it!" Though he didn't feel it, he tried to sound confident.

“Young man,” Key replied with a forced smile, “if you are right, then September 14, 1814, will be one of the most remembered days in our nation’s history.”

As the night fell, the peaceful calm ended, and the guns roared. For hours the darkness was alive with the sounds of war. Rockets lit up the skies, their bright flashes revealing the frantic activities of men on the shore and in the bay. Amid the sounds of cannon fire and rifle shots were the frenzied calls of the injured pleading for help. There was fire everywhere. Never had Nathan witnessed such destruction or terror.

The men serving on Nathan’s frigate were gathered on the deck. This fight was not theirs. Prisoner exchange ships did not engage in actual combat. But these sailors could not be neutral. They paced the deck, rooting for their own country.

Each time the Fort McHenry cannons fired, cheers filled the air. When the American forces scored a direct hit, the men slapped each other on the back. But each time the British forces found their targets, the men groaned and muttered softly. No one slept that night, and few remained calm.

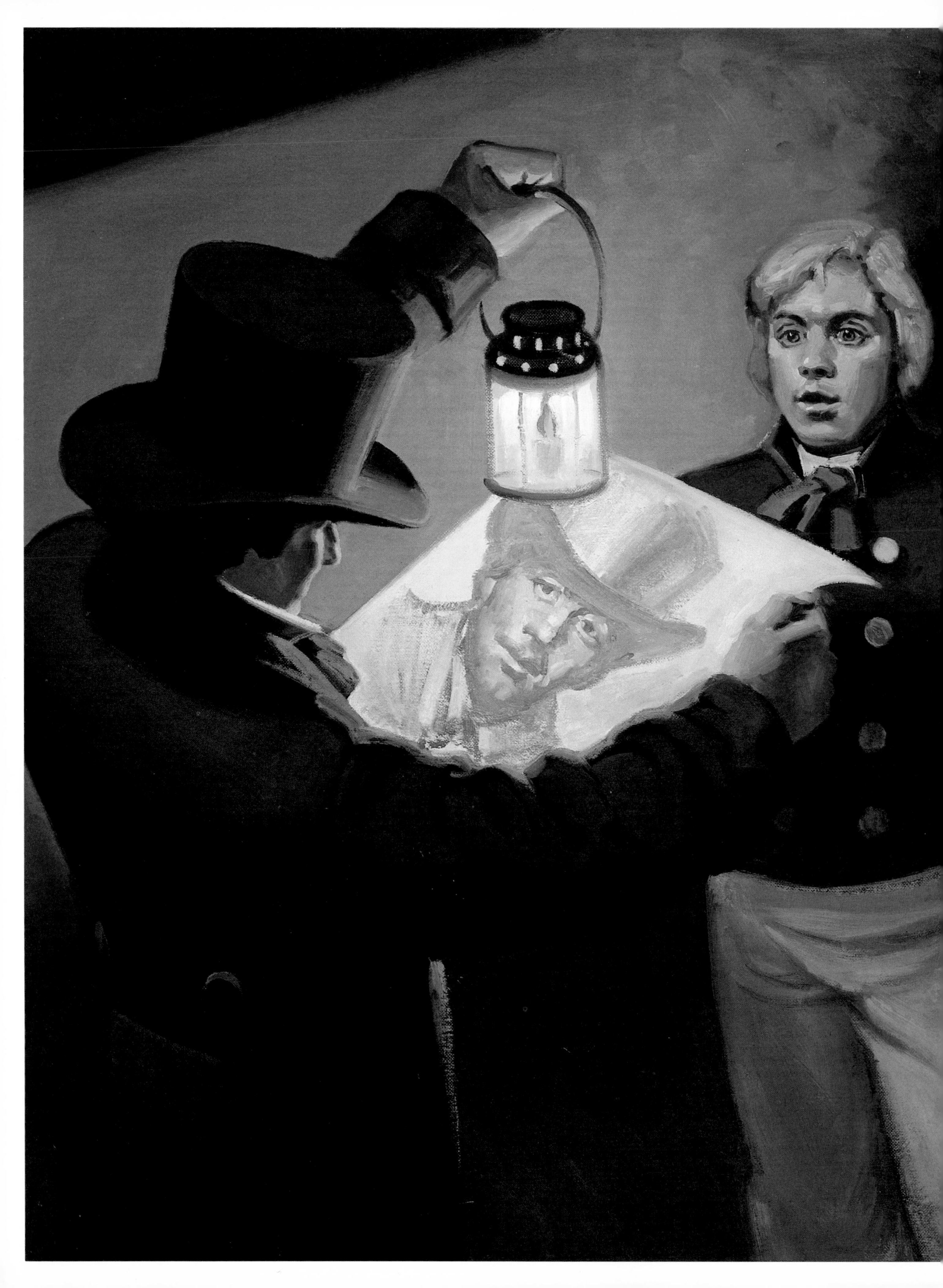

"Are you still drawing?" Key asked Nathan as the night wore on.

"Mainly I am watching, sir," the lad explained. "It's too dark for me to make out the details I need to do a good job. But I did manage to finish one a while ago. Would you like to see it?"

"Yes, I would," the gentleman answered. Nathan turned and retrieved a leather pouch from the deck. From it he pulled a large piece of paper. Taking it from the boy, Key held it up to a lantern. As he surveyed it, the man's eyebrows lifted with pride. "This is a drawing of me!"

"Yes, sir," Nathan answered. "I drew you while you were standing beside the rail watching the battle. I hope you like it. You can see the fort in the background."

"I like it very much," Key returned, a note of admiration in his voice. "I do believe that you have drawn me a bit better looking than I really am." Walking across to the middle of the deck, the man took a seat beside Nathan. "Tell me about yourself."

"My parents were third generation Americans," the lad began, proudly. "My grandfather fought at Valley Forge with President Washington. My father was a teacher. He had a college education, and he even visited the Louisiana Territory once.

"Mother was beautiful, and she taught me how to draw things. She was really much better at this than I am."

"What happened to your parents?" inquired Key.

"They died about three years ago," Nathan explained sadly. "It was winter, and they got sick. When they died, I didn't have anyone else, so my neighbor took me to Mr. Chapman. He's an officer in the navy, and he took me on as a cabin boy. Now Mr. Chapman takes care of me. I was so sad in the beginning, but now I love being at sea. And I have gotten to sail everywhere!"

"I am sure you have," the man smiled.

"Once," Nathan whispered excitedly, "I got to spend a whole week on our new ship, the U.S.S. Constitution. The British Navy couldn't touch her. Still can't. I even met Captain John Paul Jones!"

"Then you *have* been lucky," Key laughed. "You said your father was a teacher. Where did he go to college?"

"St. Mary's," came the lad's quick reply.

"Was his first name Wylie?"

"Yes, sir," an astonished Nathan answered. "How did you know?"

"He and I were in school together," the man explained. "He was a good man, and you look like him. If I remember correctly, he once told me that your grandfather knew the great American hero, Nathan Hale."

"I was named for him," Nathan exclaimed. "Sir, if I may ask, why are you here?"

Surprised by the lad's curiosity, the man scratched his head thoughtfully. "It is not really a very exciting story," Mr. Key smiled. "Are you sure you want to hear it?"

Nodding, Nathan waited.

"A friend of mine," he began, "Dr. William Beanes, was being held captive by the British. I approached President Madison for permission to petition the enemy for his release. I am an attorney, and I thought I might be able to use my legal training in the matter.

"The president was very upset. He had good reason. The English have conducted themselves in this war in a manner not befitting civilized men. I was there when they burned Washington, D.C., and that is when they unlawfully kidnapped Dr. Beanes. It took me some time, but I convinced the president that my taking a chance to win the freedom of one of this nation's great doctors was worth the risk. Yet, he insisted on sending one of his men with me when I met with the British Admiral Cockburn. That was Colonel Skinner – you have probably noticed him walking around the deck. After many days and much negotiating, we managed to obtain the doctor's freedom.

"Now, with my job finished, I am stuck helpless on this ship, while my family is ashore. Now I watch the enemy pound the city where my grandfather, John Ross Key, lived when he first came to this land."

Taking a deep breath, he rose and walked back to watch the battle. The thoughts of his wife and children seemed to have left him heavy-hearted. Yet, it was obvious to Nathan that this man placed duty to his country before anything else. If it were for the United States, then there was nothing else he could do. Only God, it seemed, came before his country.

"I see you have come to know our guest," George Chapman remarked as he passed by to check the front rigging.

"He is a nice man," Nathan answered.

"We need more like him," George replied.

Suddenly a sharp blast echoed through the darkness. An errant cannon ball came flying through the night and struck the ship's main rigging. Rope and wood rained down onto the deck and into the bay, sending men scurrying for cover. As burning sail cloth lit up the night, Nathan watched the American flag fall from the mast and float out over the water.

The lad rushed across the deck and looked out into the bay. The once proud red, white, and blue banner was now heading toward a watery grave. Without thinking, Nathan jumped up onto the rail and plunged into the dark waters.

Deep below the surface he dove, far under fallen lumber and lines, trying to hold his breath until he was clear of all the debris. His lungs burned as he fought past a torn sail and neared the surface. But just before he could taste the sweetness of life-giving air, one of the broken and twisted lines caught around his ankle.

He jerked mightily, but it held him fast. Reaching back with his right hand, he found the rope and tried to slip it over his boot, but he just wasn't strong enough. Thrashing, his chest crushed from the lack of oxygen, Nathan forced his left hand down beside his right and used both in a last effort to pull himself free. Just when he thought his lungs would explode, the line gave way and his head burst through the water's surface.

Gasping for air, Nathan looked around in the bay. Finally he caught sight of the flag floating ten yards away. By now Chapman, Key, and all the men on the ship had spotted Nathan in the water. As he swam toward the flag, they realized what he was doing. Cheering, they urged him on. Just as Nathan grabbed the flag, Chapman tossed him a line. As Nathan held onto it, Chapman pulled him through the sea and back onto the ship.

"Permission to come aboard," a very wet Nathan said as he was hauled over the rail.

"Granted," the captain replied.

"Here's our flag," the young man declared proudly, handing the drenched banner to the officer.

"Chapman," the captain ordered, "put this back where it belongs."

As the officer raised the flag, Nathan walked to the rail, still panting and now beginning to feel cold.

"You are a brave one," Key observed as Nathan approached him. "I will tell President Madison what you have done. He will want to meet you."

Nathan smiled proudly.

"You know, Nathan," Key went on, "I told you that I knew your father in college. Well, he was a thoughtful man who loved this country and the ideals it represented. He often talked about how fortunate we were to live in a nation where the people ruled, where we made our own choices. He told me that he hoped that, when he had children, they would recognize how special it was to be a part of these great United States. I think tonight you would have made him very proud."

Nathan felt happy and sad, all at the same time. He tried to speak to thank Mr. Key, but his voice was stuck in his throat.

Key didn't seem to notice. Shaking his head, he looked back toward the city and sighed, "I pray that we can hold off the enemy and maintain this nation for you and your children. On this very night, the fate of all of us hangs in the balance."

"You are a great man, Mr. Key," Nathan answered. "You have such love for this land."

Grinning, the man put his hand on Nathan's shoulder, looked back toward the first rays of a new day, and shook his head. "I am but a simple lawyer, a husband and a father. I do what I must, write a few verses of poetry to entertain my children and pass the time, and leave the real work of heroes to greater men. I will be quickly forgotten, but . . . ."

He paused in midthought, his blue eyes squinting as the early light of dawn broke over the sea. The fort, the site of last night's fierce battle, could just be seen through the morning mist. Peering through the smoke and haze, Key tried to see what the long fight had done to the American port.

"Nathan," the man urged, "I cannot see our fort. But you are young. Your eyes are better than mine. Tell me what you see!"

Searching in the early light of dawn, Nathan studied the area around the fort. There was so much haze, so little light, and it was so far away. But finally, out of the

shadows, above the smoke and flames, it appeared. Just visible, tattered but still waving, was the American flag.

"The flag!" Nathan screamed, his heart pounding wildly. "Look everyone, our flag is still there!"

The whole crew raced to the side of the ship. Staring breathlessly, they pointed one by one to the red, white, and blue banner. Cheers erupted, the men cried, laughed, and hugged each other, and prayers were offered. As a nation, America had survived for one more night.

George Chapman sought out Nathan and lifted him off the deck. As he swung him round and round, he yelled, "They couldn't take us and they never will!" Putting the lad down on the deck, he ran up to the captain, who for the moment had forgotten his rank and was celebrating with the enlisted men. Never had Nathan seen such excitement and joy.

Looking back toward the fort, he saw Key still standing by the rail looking out toward the shore. Forgetting the celebration that had broken out all around him, Nathan went to stand beside the tall man. As he did, he heard Key whispering.

"Oh, say, can you see, by the dawn's early light, what so proudly we hailed at the twilight's last gleaming, whose broad stripes and bright stars, through the perilous fight, o'er the ramparts we watched, were so gallantly streaming?"

As the man paused, Nathan asked, "What are those words? I've never heard them."

Key answered, "These are the words that are in my heart at this moment."

"You should write them down," Nathan earnestly observed. "I would like a copy of them."

"You are too kind," the man smiled. "I am just a poor excuse for a poet. My words only serve to say what is in my heart."

"But they also say what is in mine," Nathan responded. "You should save them."

"I have no ink or quill," Key explained.

Dashing across the deck, Nathan retrieved his writing instruments from his case. Returning, he handed them to the man.

Francis Scott Key turned back to study the tattered banner that still flew over the heavily damaged fort. Drawing an old letter from his pocket, Key slowly dipped the pen in ink and began to write. Minutes later, he looked up and handed the poem to Nathan. Nathan slowly read its words.

Just as he finished, George Chapman walked up.

"Another one of your drawings?" he asked.

"No," Nathan answered. "Some special words that Mr. Key wrote about the battle. Listen: 'Oh, say, does that star-spangled banner yet wave o'er the land of the free, and the home of the brave?'"

Looking toward Key the lad exclaimed, "Yes, it does!" He gave the letter back to the man.

"Mr. Key," he asked, "what will you do with your poem?"

"I don't know," Key laughed. "Maybe read it to my children."

A few hours later Francis Scott Key boarded a boat that took him back to shore. That morning, in a Baltimore hotel, he rewrote his rough draft of "The Star-Spangled Banner." Eventually, he read it to his children.

A few months later, after the war had ended and a peace treaty had been signed, Nathan Dunn stood on the ground of the Boston Commons. Mr. Francis Scott Key and his family were just behind him; George Chapman was at his side. Hundreds of others encircled the group on all sides. Directly in front of Nathan stood President James Madison.

"Nathan Dunn," the president proudly began, "we are here to give you this medal of valor. You have earned this recognition because you willingly risked your life to save the symbol of all that we hold dear. This nation is deeply indebted to you. As long as young people believe in this land, as you have shown that you do, we will remain a free people.

"Now," President Madison continued after pinning the medal on Nathan's chest, "I would like you to take this flag, the same one you pulled from the bay the morning of September 14, and run it up the flag pole."

Taking the banner in hand, Nathan proudly walked to the pole, hooked the line into the flag, and raised it to its highest point. Then, stepping back, he saluted. As he did, a military band began to play.

As the music sounded, the hundreds who were gathered looked down at freshly printed sheets of paper and began to sing the words that were written there. But Nathan didn't have to read the words. He was there the morning that Francis Scott Key wrote "The Star-Spangled Banner." He already knew the words by heart.

*The first Independence Day celebration
was held on July 4, 1777, in Philadelphia.
This was one year and two days after
the Declaration of Independence
was signed and exactly one year after
it was first read to the people
of the American colonies.
An elaborate post-Revolutionary War
celebration was held
in Philadelphia in 1788.
Since then the day has been marked
annually with fireworks,
picnics, speeches, patriotic music,
and the displaying of the
red, white, and blue colors.
Since 1931 "The Star-Spangled Banner"
has been this nation's official anthem.*